Welcome to
Hopscotch Hill School!
In Miss Sparks's class,
you will make friends
with children just like you.
They love school,
and they love to learn!
Keep an eye out for Razzi,
the class pet rabbit.
He may be anywhere!
See if you can spot him
as you read the story.

Welcome!

Miss Sparks

Hallie

Razzi

Logan

Skylar

Avery

Spencer

Nathan

Gwen

Lindy

Delaney

Connor

ISBN 0-439-68582-6

Copyright © 2003 by Pleasant Company. All rights reserved.
Published by Scholastic Inc., 557 Broadway, New York, NY 10012,
by arrangement with Pleasant Company Publications. SCHOLASTIC and associated logos
are trademarks and/or registered trademarks of Scholastic Inc.

12 11 10 9 8 7 6 5 4 3   4 5 6 7 8 9/0

Printed in the U.S.A.   23

First Scholastic printing, September 2004

Visit our website at www.americangirl.com
Hopscotch Hill School™ and logo, Hopscotch Hill™, Where a love for learning grows™,
Hallie™, and American Girl® are trademarks of Pleasant Company.

American Girl®

Hallie's Horrible Handwriting

by Valerie Tripp illustrated by Joy Allen

SCHOLASTIC INC.

New York Toronto London Auckland Sydney
Mexico City New Delhi Hong Kong Buenos Aires

Things with Wings

Sunshine made
Miss Sparks's classroom
bright and warm.
"Boys and girls,"
said Miss Sparks.
"Look at Hallie's drawing."
"Oooh," said the children.
Hallie smiled shyly.
"Hallie," said Miss Sparks,
"please tell us why you drew
fairies and butterflies."
Hallie spoke softly and slowly.
She said, "I think things
with wings are pretty."
"So do I," said Miss Sparks.
The sparkles on her glasses glittered.

It was the second day of school.

Hallie already loved her teacher.

Miss Sparks reminded Hallie

of a good fairy.

Her classroom was like

something in a fairy tale, too.

The floor was painted green like grass.

A big tree seemed to grow in a corner.

Sunlight danced on the walls.

There was a rainbow of counting beads
below the chalkboard.
The ceiling was painted blue
with puffy white clouds.
It looked just like the real sky.
Hallie was sure that Miss Sparks's
classroom was the nicest classroom
in Hopscotch Hill School.
And Miss Sparks was the nicest teacher.

Hallie wanted to follow

Miss Sparks's rules for the class:

1. We take turns.

2. We listen when others talk.

3. We raise our hands

when we have something to say.

Hallie saw her friend Logan

raise her hand.

Logan said, "Look, Miss Sparks!

The rabbit's cage is empty!"

Miss Sparks smiled.

She said, "Razzi is our pet rabbit.

He does not like to stay in his hutch.

You may spot him anywhere!"

The class was delighted.

Spencer hopped around the room
pretending that he was a rabbit.

"I bet I will find Razzi!" said Spencer.

"Perhaps," said Miss Sparks.

"But usually a child who can be quiet
sees Razzi first."

"Then I will act like a carrot!"
joked Spencer.

Everyone laughed at Spencer.

But Hallie saw that Miss Sparks

was smiling straight at her.

Right then, Hallie made up her mind.

She would be quiet.

Then she would spot the rabbit.

She would always do her best work.

Then she would please Miss Sparks.

Miss Sparks handed back

everyone's drawings.

"Class," she said, "fold your drawings

in half to make little tents."

Miss Sparks gave everyone

a piece of lined paper

and a pencil

with a pink eraser on it.

12

"Write your name," said Miss Sparks.

"Then glue it to your drawing.

It will be a name card for your desk."

"Oh, no," thought Hallie.

She knew how to spell her name.

But Hallie did not like writing.

Slowly, she picked up her pencil.

Slowly, she started to write an **H.**

Oops! The middle of the **H** caved in.

It looked as if it had a stomach ache.

Hallie erased it and looked around.

Some children were already

gluing their names to their drawings!

Skylar was helping Logan.

Spencer was wearing his name card

on his head like a hat.

Hallie had an ache in her middle,

just like her **H.**

The ache got worse

when she wrote another **H.**

The lines touched at the top like an **A.**

Hallie was in such a rush that

she left the **A** and put an **H** in front of it.

"Hallie," Miss Sparks said kindly,

"we do not write in all uppercase.

Please use lowercase letters, too."

"Yes, Miss Sparks," said Hallie.

She erased the **A.**

The other children were taking turns

sharing their name cards with the class.

But Hallie could not look up.

She had to finish in a hurry.

Finally, Hallie was done.

Her name looked horrible!

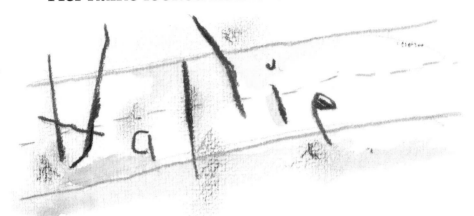

Sadly, Hallie glued her name

to her drawing.

When it was her turn to share,

Hallie held her name card down low.

She hoped that no one could see it.

"How come your **e**

is so squashed?" asked Skylar.

Hallie's face felt hot.

She was too ashamed to speak.

Miss Sparks said, "Everyone's letters
look a little different, Skylar.
Thank you, Hallie. You may sit down."
Hallie was sure that Miss Sparks
was disappointed in her name card.
The sparkles on Miss Sparks's glasses
were not glittering at all.

A Pupa Project

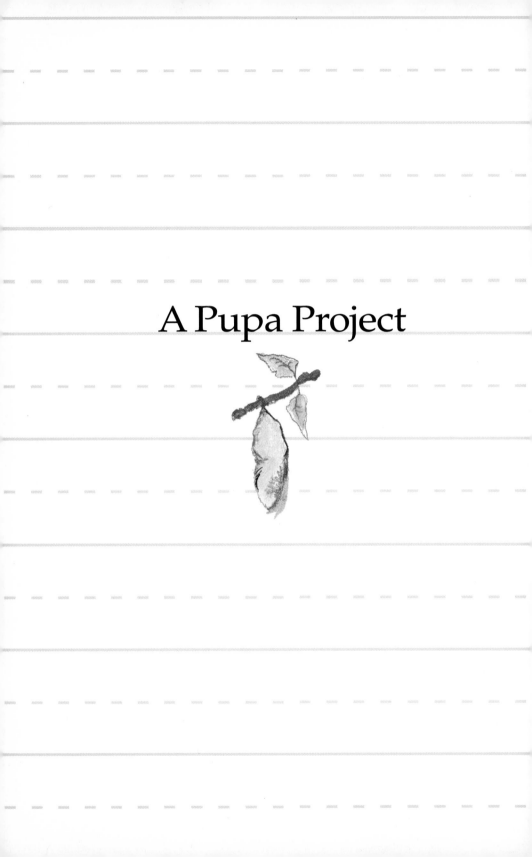

Except for horrible handwriting,

Hallie loved school more every day.

Except for her horrible name card,

Hallie loved everything in the classroom.

Hallie loved to read in the bathtub.

She loved to wear the butterfly wings

from the dress-up closet.

She loved to be quiet and find Razzi.

Hallie loved Miss Sparks

more and more, too.

One morning, Miss Sparks said,
"We are going to begin
a pupa project today.
Hallie, I bet you can tell us
what a pupa is."
Hallie smiled and nodded.
Hallie said, "A pupa
turns into a butterfly."

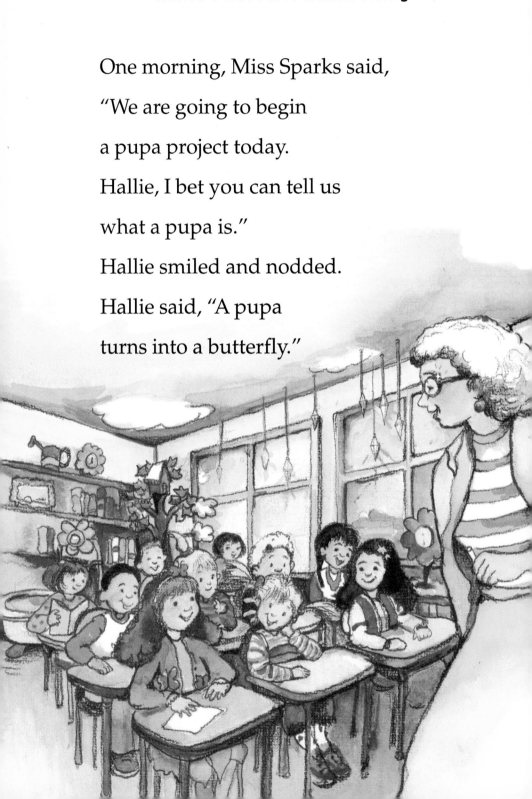

"That's right," said Miss Sparks.

"Each one of you will be

given a pupa to care for."

The children were excited.

Hallie was thrilled!

But then Miss Sparks said,

"Caring for a pupa is a big job.

Every day, you will write in

your journal about your pupa."

Oh, no! So much writing!

Hallie's heart sank.

Miss Sparks wrote **pupa**

and **butterfly** on the board.

She said, "Copy these words."

Slowly, Hallie opened her journal.

Slowly, she lifted her pencil.

Slowly, she began to write.

Oh, dear!

Some of Hallie's letters were too tall.

Some were too short.

Some were too fat. Some were too thin.

Miss Sparks was very nice about it.

She said, "All you need is practice."

But Hallie hated handwriting.

She never wanted to practice.

Every day, Miss Sparks wrote

a list of words for the children to copy.

Every day, Hallie's journal was a mess.

She had to erase so much!

She always had to rush!

One day, Miss Sparks wrote

a whole sentence to copy.

Hallie tried hard, but her sentence

looked terrible.

Her words banged into each other.

Her words swooped up

above the lines and fell down below.

With a sigh, Hallie began to erase.

She rubbed too hard.

The page in her journal tore.

Suddenly, something tore

inside of Hallie, too.

She could not stand handwriting

another second!

Hallie slammed her pencil onto her desk.

She ripped the ruined page

out of her journal.

She wadded the page into a ball.

She threw it as hard as she could.

The paper bounced off her desk.

Hallie jumped to her feet.

"I hate handwriting!" she cried out.

"It's too hard! I can't do it!"

Then Hallie sat down hard.

She burst into tears.

Everyone felt terrible

to see her so upset.

Other children began to cry, too.

Hallie sobbed and sobbed.

She felt Miss Sparks's hand

on her shoulder.

"Hallie, dear," said Miss Sparks.

"I am sorry this is so hard for you.

Everything will be all right.

You will see."

But Hallie knew things would NOT

be all right.

Not ever again.

All because of horrible handwriting!

Flutter By, Butterflies!

Hallie felt very sad the next day.
She was sure that she had
disappointed Miss Sparks.
But when Hallie walked
into the classroom,
Miss Sparks was smiling.
She said,
"Good morning, Hallie."
Hallie started to say,
"Good morning."
Then she stopped.

She saw the most surprising thing.
There was a butterfly on her desk!
Hallie looked at Miss Sparks.
Miss Sparks shrugged.
She said, "I don't know where it came from."

Hallie walked to her desk.

The butterfly was made out of paper.

It was attached to a pencil

as if it had landed there to stay.

Very gently, Hallie lifted the pencil.

The butterfly's wings opened up

just like a real butterfly's wings.

The butterfly's wings seemed

to make the pencil lighter.

Very carefully, Hallie wrote:

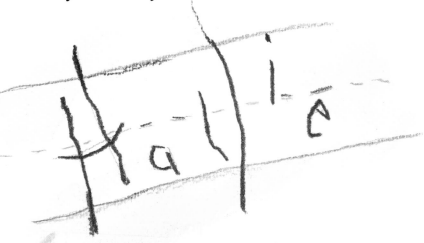

She smiled. Her name did not look so bad!

That day, Hallie did not mind

handwriting so much.

She still had to erase a lot,

but she did not mind that either.

She liked the way the wings on the pencil

fluttered when she erased.

The next day Hallie found

two sheets of paper on her desk.

One sheet had a border of butterflies.

The other sheet had a border of ladybugs

and a message that said,

"Keep trying, Hallie!"

The message made Hallie smile

because it was so nice.

The next day Hallie found a note

in her pocket that said,

"Your letters will get better."

Hallie loved the secret surprises.

They were like gifts

that good fairies might leave.

It cheered her up to have

such kind friends in her class.

Hallie saw that the writing

on the notes wasn't perfect.

She realized that she was not

the only one in the class

having trouble with handwriting.

Hallie took the pretty paper

and the butterfly pencil home.

She liked using them so

much that she practiced

writing her name

over and over again.

33

Hallie's letters still wiggled

above and below the lines.

But with the friendly ladybugs

and butterflies around them,

Hallie didn't mind the wiggles so much.

A few weeks later,

Miss Sparks said, "Boys and girls,

soon our butterflies will hatch.

We will set them free.

Someone needs to make

a good-bye card that we can all sign.

I think Hallie should make the card.

Do you think so, too?"

"Yes!" said everyone.

"Oh, no . . ." Hallie began to say.

Then she saw Miss Sparks smiling at her.

The sparkles on Miss Sparks's glasses

glittered like fairy dust.

Hallie smiled. She said, "I will do it."

Making the good-bye card was a hard job.

Hallie had to erase

and start again many times.

Even so, the letters were never perfect.

But Hallie had a good idea.

When a letter sagged below the line,

Hallie drew a fat butterfly sitting on it.

When a letter rose up above the line,

she drew a butterfly over it, lifting it up.

Soon the day came to set the butterflies free.

Everyone signed the back of the card.

Miss Sparks led the class outside.

Hallie was wearing the butterfly wings

from the dress-up closet.

Hallie hopped to make the wings flutter.

Miss Sparks said, "Boys and girls,

this is a sad day because

we're going to say good-bye

to our butterflies.

But it is a happy day, too, because

we know they will be happy

to be free. Ready, children?"

"Yes!" said everyone.

Miss Sparks opened the box.

The butterflies flew

up into the air.

"Oooh," sighed the children.

Hallie tilted her head back.

The butterflies looked like

fairies dancing in the sky.

Miss Sparks stood
behind Hallie.
They watched the butterflies
fly into the high blue sky.
"Look, Hallie,"
said Miss Sparks.
"See how the butterflies fly?
They do not fly in a straight line.
It may take them a while.
But they will get to where
they want to be.
Your handwriting will get
where you want it to be too."
Hallie began to think that maybe,
just maybe, it would.

"Good-bye!" the children called

to the butterflies.

Hallie held up the good-bye card.

She liked the way the message looked,

looping and swooping,

just like the butterflies

now that they were free.

Dear Parents . . .

Is handwriting—or addition, or reading—horribly hard for your child? Like Hallie, most children have trouble with at least *one* new skill. They are frustrated. They feel rushed. They compare themselves to their classmates and feel they are not as good.

How can you smooth some of the frustration out of learning new skills? The following activities, suggested by the Hopscotch Hill School advisory board, are designed to help children learn by using their skills and their senses. Most of all, the activities tap into your child's sense of *fun*.

All Writing's All Right!

Sometimes small hands like Hallie's just aren't ready to handle a pencil. But who says pencil and paper are necessary to practice writing? Try these ways instead:

- Let your child **trace letters with her finger** on your back, and try to guess what she wrote. Then trace letters on her back, and see if she can identify them. (Tickling is allowed!)

- Spray a circle of shaving cream on a plastic table-cloth, and let your child **finger-paint letters** in the cream.

- Help your child **make three-dimensional letters** out of Play-Doh, clay, or bread dough.

Dear Parents . . .

- Show your child how to **form letters using her whole body** while lying on the floor or standing.

- Next time you're at the beach, let your child **write in wet sand** with her finger or a long stick.

- Let your child **"write" with a flashlight** outside at night or on the walls of a darkened room.

- Give your child a squirt gun or hose so that she can **write with water** on the driveway or sidewalk.

- Let your child **write on pavement** with fat pieces of chalk or a large paintbrush and water.

- Encourage your child to **add sound effects** while writing at home, such as whistling down the slope of an *N* or sounding a *ding!* when dotting an *i*.

- **Compare letters to other things**, such as animals. Ask your child, "What animal has humps like an *m*?"

- Let your child **pretend to be the teacher**, teaching *you*—or her dolls—how to write letters.

Right on Time

Sometimes children like Hallie feel rushed at school. It's time to line up for lunch, and your daughter hasn't finished her drawing yet! How can you help her feel more comfortable with her school schedule?

• Chat with your child about what activities she does during the school day. Ask her to draw pictures or cut pictures out of a magazine that show children doing those activities. **Make a school day collage** of the pictures, and hang it in your child's room. Use it to talk about how the activities *begin* and *end*. Ask, "Which activity came first today?" "Which is usually last?" "Which lasts the longest?" "Is recess before or after lunch?"

- **Make a collage of home activities,** too. Chat with your child about it. Ask, "What do we do before school?" "What do we do before dinner?" "What do we do on Saturday morning?"

- When you're playing a game, **use an egg timer** or oven timer to teach your child about "stop" times. When the timer dings, it's time for someone else's turn or time to move on to another activity. Or **play some of your child's favorite music** when she is playing a game, and explain to her that when the music ends, it will be time to *stop*.

- Use words such as "It's time to . . ." or "Time's up!" when a switch in activity has to take place quickly. Remind your child that she can return to her activity at another time. Be specific. Say, "You can finish this drawing after dinner." Be sure to **let her know how helpful she is** when she switches to a new task without a fuss.

Look What I Can Do!

Is your child a whiz at puzzles? Does she sing songs all day? Is she a wiggle-worm or a bookworm? You know your child's strengths. Help *her* get to know them, too. Here's how:

• Divide a large piece of posterboard in two. Label the left side Things I Can Do Easily. Label the right side Things I Am Learning How to Do. Help your child put drawings or photographs under the headings. Celebrate when it's time to move one from the right to the left!

• Chat with your child about something she has gotten better at over time, such as putting together puzzles. Praise her and remind her that things that are hard for her now will get easier as she gets older and bigger and has more practice with them.

- Say things like "I'll give this a try" or "Trying this will be fun" so that your child can see you **try new things** and will have language to use herself when she's trying something new.

- **Don't hide your mistakes!** Talk and laugh about your own boo-boos so that your child will feel comfortable taking risks and making mistakes, too.

- Save photos, school certificates, notes from teachers, and other items highlighting accomplishments in your child's life. **Look through these treasures** with your child, and talk about how much she has done and changed.

- **Celebrate** the fact that everyone is good at doing different things. Talk about how the different people in your family have **different talents.**

Hallie's Horrible Handwriting and the activities that follow the story were developed with guidance from the Hopscotch Hill School advisory board:

Dominic Gullo is a professor of Early Childhood Education at Queens College, City University of New York. He is a member of the governing board of the National Association for the Education of Young Children, and he is a consultant to school districts across the country in the areas of early childhood education, curriculum, and assessment.

Margaret Jensen has taught beginning reading for 32 years and is currently a math resource teacher in the Madison Metropolitan School District, Wisconsin. She has served on committees for the International Reading Association and the Wisconsin State Reading Association, and has been president of the Madison Area Reading Council. She has presented at workshops and conferences in the areas of reading, writing, and children's literature.

Kim Miller is a school psychologist at Lowell Elementary in Madison, Wisconsin, where she works with children, parents, and teachers to help solve—and prevent—problems related to learning and adjustment to the classroom setting.

Virginia Pickerell has worked with teachers and parents as an educational consultant and counselor within the Madison Metropolitan School District. She has researched and presented workshops on topics such as learning processes, problem solving, and creativity. She is also a former director of Head Start.

Free catalogue!

If your own spirited student enjoys this book,
she'll love exploring the American Girl® catalogue.
It features the growing world of Hopscotch Hill
School books, dolls, and playthings, along with
Bitty Baby® and the Bitty Twins®!

To receive your free catalogue, return this card,
visit our Web site at americangirl.com, or call
1-800-845-0005.

Send me a catalogue:

_____ / / _____
Name   Girl's birth date

_____
Address

_____
City   State   Zip

_____
E-mail *(Fill in to receive order information, updates, and Web-exclusive offers.)*

(_____)
Phone ❏ Home ❏ Work

_____
Parent's signature   12583i

Send my friend a catalogue:

_____
Name

_____
Address

_____
City   State   Zip

                                      12591i

Place
Stamp
Here

American Girl ®

PO BOX 620497
MIDDLETON WI 53562-0497